The Young Philosophers of Athens

By L. R. Caldwell

Published by Reason and Reality Publishing
Florida, United States

ISBN: **979-8-9992710-9-9**

Printed in the United States of America

Cover and Interior Design by L. R. Caldwell

Dedication

To the Teachers who have the wisdom to answer questions with deeper questions.

To the children who will ask questions. Finding answers even in the silence. Understanding that age does not determine the wisdom one holds.

Knowing that answers can be questions within themselves.

Table of Contents

Preface

Long before the world called them philosophers, three boys once played beneath the same Grecian sun.
They raced through olive groves, argued by wells, and asked the kinds of questions that still stir in young hearts today—questions about truth, courage, kindness, and what it really means to be good.

This book tells their story before they became famous names in history.
Here, Socrates, Plato, and Aristotle are not marble statues or distant teachers.

They are children—curious, stubborn, and full of wonder—learning that wisdom does not begin in temples or scrolls, but in everyday moments: a broken toy, a spilled bucket, a runaway goat, or the quiet beauty of a setting sun.

Each chapter opens a small doorway into that world, where thought and feeling meet.

Through the laughter, mistakes, and discoveries of these three friends, readers are invited to listen closely—to see that philosophy is not something far away or difficult. It lives wherever people think honestly, care deeply, and try to understand one another.

For students, may these pages remind you that every question has value, even the ones that seem minor. For teachers, may they serve as gentle sparks to help young minds find their own voices among the ancient ones.

And for everyone who turns these pages, may you discover what the boys of Athens began to learn—that the most incredible wisdom often hides in the simplest moments, waiting to be seen by anyone who still knows how to question.

Chapter 1

The Game of Shadows

The Afternoon on the Hill

The sunlight played tricks on the mind that day, turning boys into giants and stones into secrets. Plato knelt in the dust, drawing circles with a broken twig, while Aristotle darted around nearby, chasing a lizard that vanished into a crack between the rocks. The smell of crushed thyme drifted through the air, and the cicadas sang as if the world itself were awake and curious about the boy's actions.

The Shadow Game Begins

It began as a game. Plato noticed how his shadow stretched across the ground, tall and thin, the head wobbling with each tilt. 'Look!' he laughed. 'It copies everything I do, but never perfectly.'

Socrates, sitting quietly on a nearby stone, tilted his head. 'Do you think the shadow is real, or only pretending to be you?'

Aristotle jumped beside his own dark outline. 'Of course it's real—it moves when I move!'

A Simple Experiment

They began to test the mystery. Aristotle climbed onto a large stone and raised his arm. The shadow followed. He stepped down, and the shadow shrank. 'It obeys me,' he said proudly.

Socrates smiled. 'Then who do you obey when you move?'

The question hung between them like dust in sunlight.

The Disagreement

Plato, tracing another shape in the dirt, frowned. 'Maybe the shadow is the truer one—it isn't trapped in dust or weight.'

Aristotle shook his head. 'It's nothing but less light!' He kicked a pebble, scattering the fine powder around their feet.

Socrates watched them. 'Maybe truth is not in the shadow or the stone,' he said softly, 'but in the seeing.'

The Moment of Stillness

As the sun lowered, the world turned golden. The boys sat beneath an olive tree where the air smelled of sap and soil. Their shadows grew longer, then thinner, then vanished into the coming dusk.

Plato whispered, 'If the shadows vanish, does that mean the truth is gone?'

Socrates looked at the fading horizon. 'No,' he said, 'only that we'll need a new kind of light to see it.'

Closing Reflection

Later, when the storyteller would recall this day, he would say that the boys thought they were chasing shadows. But perhaps it was the shadows that had begun chasing them—the questions, the wonder, and the light that never left their hearts.

Chapter 2

The Broken Toy

The Morning Accident

The sound of breaking clay was sharper than any argument the boys had ever had.

Aristotle froze, staring at the shattered pieces of his favorite toy, a miniature horse, painted once in bright blue and red, now scattered across the stone courtyard.

The lizard he had been chasing darted away, leaving only silence and the dusty smell of sun-baked earth. He sank to his knees, gathering the broken pieces, his small hands trembling.

Plato and Socrates exchanged glances but said nothing. The cicadas droned above them, indifferent to sorrow.

The Argument of Value

'It's ruined,' Aristotle muttered, his voice shaking. 'My father gave it to me as a gift when I learned to write my name.'

Plato crouched beside him, studying the fragments. 'It's still beautiful,' he said softly. 'Maybe more so now— it's lived a story.'

Aristotle frowned. 'A broken story.'

4

Socrates picked up one of the larger pieces, turning it in the light. 'Does its meaning vanish when its shape does?' he asked. 'Or does it still carry what it once was?'

Aristotle looked away. 'A broken horse is no horse at all.'

Plato smiled faintly. 'Then perhaps beauty isn't in the clay but in the remembering.'

An Experiment in Repair

They gathered the pieces, arranging them on a flat stone. The air was thick with the scent of olive oil and dust.

Plato fetched a small pot of resin from his home, and together they began fitting the shards like a puzzle.

Aristotle's brow furrowed in concentration as he pressed two edges together, the resin glistening in the sun.

'If we mend it,' Plato said, 'will it be the same horse?'

Aristotle sighed. 'No. It will be proof that I was clumsy.'

Socrates smiled. 'Or proof that you cared enough to mend what you broke.'

Their laughter returned slowly, mixed with the stickiness of the glue and the clumsy dance of repair. When they finished, the little horse stood crooked but whole, its scars shining like tiny rivers of gold.

The Visit to the Potter's Stall
Later that day, they carried the mended horse through the crowded marketplace.

The air was filled with the smell of baked bread and the calls of merchants.

They stopped at the stall of an old potter, his hands dark with clay and wisdom.

'Can it be fixed better?' Aristotle asked, holding up the toy.

The potter chuckled. 'Fixed? It already is. Even the earth remembers every crack. What's broken teaches the hands that shape it.'

Socrates nodded thoughtfully. 'So the break has value, then.'

'More than you think,' the potter replied. 'It tells the story of how something learned to endure.'

Evening Reflection by the Sea

By evening, the boys walked home along the sea. The air was cool and calmer now, and waves silently whispered against the shore.

Aristotle held the mended toy close to his chest. Its cracks caught the fading light like threads of amber.

Plato skipped a stone across the water. 'Maybe things don't stay whole because they're meant to be shared.'

Socrates smiled. 'Or because we learn more from mending than from perfection.'

They walked in silence after that, each step leaving small prints in the damp sand. Behind them, the sea washed their footprints away, but the warmth between them remained.

Closing Reflection

That night, as lamplight flickered across the small home, the horse stood unevenly on a shelf. Its cracks gleamed where the glue had dried, turning scars into light. Aristotle fell asleep beside it, the smell of clay and oil still on his hands.

Years later, the storyteller would remember that day long after the clay had turned to dust. He would say that what was broken that morning had taught the boys something whole—that mending begins where pride ends, and that value, once seen, never truly shatters.

Chapter 3

The Argument at the Well

The Dispute at the Well

The argument began over water, but soon it was pride
that each boy was yearning for.
Two young villagers stood at the edge of the well, their
buckets clashing as they shouted.
The ropes creaked, echoing down the dark shaft, and
the smell of wet stone mixed with dust and sunlight.
A small crowd gathered, whispering—half amused,
half relieved that the noise was not their own.

Socrates was the first to step closer.
He had been walking with Plato and Aristotle, the three
of them carrying small amphorae for their families.
Plato frowned at the noise. Aristotle tilted his head,
curious.
But Socrates simply watched, calm and quiet, as if
waiting to understand the reason beneath the noise.

Socrates Steps In

"Why do you fight?" he asked the boys.
His tone was neither sharp nor mocking—just steady,

like the voice of a friend.

The older of the two glared. "He pushed his bucket ahead of mine!"
"Because I was here first!" cried the younger one, gripping the rope until his knuckles whitened.

Socrates crouched beside them, peering into the glimmering circle of water below.
"Tell me," he said, "if the well gives enough for all, what do you win by taking first?"

The older boy hesitated. "Respect," he muttered.

"Or fear?" Socrates asked softly.
The boy looked away.

Plato smiled faintly. Aristotle folded his arms. The sun beat down, and the smell of coarse hemp filled the air. The crowd's laughter faded. The quarrel had turned into something quieter—something that asked to be understood.

Beneath the Surface

Socrates gestured to the well. "See how the rope cuts a mark along your hands? The water does not ask which of you is stronger. It rises for whoever draws it."

The younger boy frowned. "But my father says men must take what is theirs."

"And do you know what is truly yours?" Socrates asked.

The boy thought for a long moment, eyes following the faint shimmer below. "My breath, perhaps," he said at last.

Socrates nodded. "Then hold fast to that. For everything else we borrow—from the earth, from each other, even from time."

Plato's gaze softened. "Then pride," he said, "is a kind of theft."

"A theft from peace," replied Socrates, "and from the self."

The Circle of Friends

After the boys walked away, embarrassed but calmer, Socrates sat beside the well.

Plato and Aristotle joined him, setting their amphorae down.

The water below shimmered with the reflection of the sky—a small piece of heaven trapped in stone.

"You ask too many questions," Aristotle said, half-teasing. "Sometimes right is just right. He was first."

"And yet," Socrates replied, "what is the use of being

first if everyone ends up angry?"

Plato leaned forward. "Maybe being right is like this water—it looks clear until we stir it."
They laughed.

Socrates picked up a pebble, dropping it into the well. The ripples spread outward, bending their reflections. "Truth," he said, "belongs to no one. It's something we draw from together, though each of us may taste it differently."

For a time, they sat in companionable silence. A heron passed overhead, its shadow gliding across the circle of light.
The villagers drifted away, their curiosity satisfied, leaving behind only the soft murmur of wind in the olive branches.

A Lesson in Reflection

The afternoon heat pressed down until even the stones seemed to hum.
Plato leaned over the edge, watching his reflection tremble in the shifting water.
"When the water shakes," he said, "the face vanishes."

Socrates nodded. "Then perhaps peace is what lets us see ourselves."

Aristotle dipped his hand in the well, splashing. "And pride is what stirs the water."

"Then pride," said Socrates, smiling, "is what blinds the soul."

They pondered that. The ripples slowly calmed until the surface became clear again.

Plato studied his own reflection. "Do you think men ever see themselves truly?"

"Only for moments," Socrates said. "Like stars between clouds."

Aristotle sighed. "Then wisdom must be patience— waiting for the clouds to pass."

Socrates chuckled. "And humility, perhaps, is learning not to chase the reflection but to steady the water."

Echoes of the Village

The sound of a goat's bell drifted from the hillside. A woman drew water nearby, glancing shyly at the three philosophers who seemed to speak to the air more than to one another.

She smiled; it was a gentle, knowing smile, as if she had heard these same questions in her own household.

Her child tugged her robe and whispered, "Mother, what do they seek?"

She answered softly, "Maybe what all men seek—

reasons for their hearts."

Socrates heard her and inclined his head, grateful. "She understands more than I," he murmured.

Return of the Younger Boy

Just as the sun began to lean westward, the younger boy returned, clutching his bucket.
He stopped a few paces from them, eyes lowered. "I shouldn't have shouted," he said. His voice was small, but it carried in the still air.

Socrates stood. "Then come draw your water. We'll help you."

Together they lowered the bucket, the rope groaning as it descended.
When the bucket came up full and cool, Socrates steadied it, letting the boy fill his jar first.

"See?" Socrates said gently. "When one hand helps another, both are filled."
The boy smiled shyly. Plato clapped him on the shoulder.

Aristotle watched the water spilling over the rim.
"Even when we share," he said, "some always spills

away."

"Yes," Socrates replied, "but what spills feeds the earth."

The boy hesitated, then asked, "Will the others laugh at me for saying sorry?"
Plato answered, "Let them.

The laughter of the unwise is lighter than dust."
Aristotle added, "Courage is not always in the fist, but in the throat that speaks first of peace."
The boy nodded, and when he turned to go, his steps were quieter, steadier.

The Long Shadow

That evening, as the sun slipped behind the olive trees, the well cast a long shadow across the path.
The boys walked home with their amphorae, water sloshing softly inside.
Behind them, the sound of the well's rope creaked once more—an echo of a day when pride had nearly outshouted reason.

Plato watched them go. "Do you think they will remember?" he asked.
Socrates smiled. "Not the words. But the feeling—that may linger, as sunlight lingers on the skin."

Aristotle rose, stretching. "Then perhaps virtue begins not in knowing, but in remembering what peace feels like."

Socrates looked toward the horizon. "And remembering to seek it again."

Closing Reflection

The storyteller, remembering it many years later, would say that wisdom often begins not in victory but in listening.

The well still stands, though the hands that quarreled are long dust.

Each morning, villagers still come to draw from it, and the echo of that old dispute hums faintly in the stone.

He would tell his listeners that truth, like water, must be drawn carefully.

If we clutch it too tightly, it slips through our fingers; if we draw it together, it cools and nourishes all.

Chapter 4

The Runaway Goat

The Escape

The morning began with laughter and the clatter of hooves.

A goat had slipped its tether near the edge of the village, where the olive groves met the rocky hill. Dust rose in clouds as it bounded toward the open fields, its bell jangling wildly.

Aristotle saw it first.
"There!" he shouted, pointing. "It's heading for the ridge!"
Plato dropped the basket he was carrying. "We should help!"
Socrates smiled. "Help the goat, or the shepherd?"

"The goat," said Aristotle without hesitation. "It looks happy."
"Or frightened," Socrates said softly. "Freedom and fear often run together."

The three boys took off across the hillside, sandals slapping against warm earth, the air full of thyme and goat bells.

The Chase

The animal darted between olive trees, nimble and quick.

Aristotle followed its path with fierce attention, noting every leap, every glance backward.

"It doesn't run straight," he observed. "It looks back before turning."

"Maybe it's thinking," said Plato.

"Or guessing," replied Aristotle. "Thinking takes time; guessing is faster."

They reached a clearing where the goat stopped near a low stone wall, sniffing the air. Its eyes were golden and watchful. For a moment, it stood perfectly still—then bolted again.

Socrates caught his breath, laughing. "Do you notice how we chase what we do not understand? We call it mischief when perhaps it is simply motion."

Aristotle crouched, studying hoofprints in the dust. "They curve, see? It isn't running away anymore. It's circling. It knows where it came from."

Plato looked toward the sunlit hills. "Then maybe the goat remembers, like people do. Maybe it longs for something even while it runs."

The Observation

They found the animal again near a stream that trickled through reeds.

It had stopped to drink, its reflection trembling in the water. The boys hid behind a boulder, whispering.

Aristotle's voice was low with excitement. "Watch how it lifts its head between sips, as if to listen. Animals learn by pattern."
"Then what do we learn from watching them?" asked Plato.
"Patience," said Socrates. "And perhaps humility. Nature rarely hurries."

The goat dipped its head once more, then looked up at them. Its eyes met theirs, not startled, but curious. For a heartbeat, all three froze.

Plato whispered, "It knows."
Aristotle shook his head. "It senses."
Socrates smiled. "And do you know the difference?"

Aristotle thought for a moment. "Sensing is like touching. Knowing is like naming."

18

"Then perhaps," said Socrates, "we name so that we may pretend to know what we have only touched."

Plato threw a pebble into the stream, sending ripples across the reflection. "Then every name is a ripple," he said.
"And every truth," Socrates added, "is what remains when the water clears again."

The Debate of Mind and Instinct

The goat wandered toward a patch of low shrubs. The boys followed slowly, their earlier haste replaced by quiet fascination.

"Maybe it isn't escaping," Plato said. "Maybe it just wanted to see more."
Aristotle frowned. "That's not reason. That's instinct."
"Is curiosity instinct?" asked Socrates.

Aristotle hesitated. "It might be. Even insects explore new ground."
Plato grinned. "Then perhaps we are all insects who learned to speak."

Socrates laughed. "If so, the gods must find us amusing, buzzing from question to question."

They stopped beneath an olive tree whose silver leaves trembled in the breeze. The goat had climbed halfway onto a low wall, balancing like an acrobat. Its bell jingled softly.

Aristotle stepped closer. "If it falls, it will hurt itself."
"Then it learns," said Socrates.

"Or it remembers next time," added Plato.
Aristotle sighed. "You both speak in circles. I just want to know how it decides what to do."

Socrates picked up a fallen twig. "Then ask not how it decides, but why you care to know."

Aristotle blinked. "Because knowing how things think helps us care for them."
"Ah," Socrates said, tapping the twig against his palm, "then you seek understanding through kindness. That is thought, not instinct."

Plato nodded. "Maybe reason begins when we care for what is not ourselves."

The Rescue

A sudden cry echoed down the hill—the shepherd's voice. "My goat! Has anyone seen my goat?"

The animal startled, jumping from the wall. Its tether, still trailing, caught on a rock. It bleated in panic, twisting its head.

The boys ran to free it.

"Easy!" Aristotle murmured, reaching for the rope. The
goat jerked away, eyes wide.
Plato circled slowly, speaking softly, almost singing.
"It's all right… You're not trapped, little one."
Socrates knelt, spreading his hands open in the dust.
"Sometimes help must wait for trust," he said quietly.

The goat stilled, breathing hard.

Aristotle moved again, slower this time. He slid his
hand along the rope until he could loosen the knot. The
moment the tension eased, the goat trembled—but did
not run.

"It understands," whispered Plato.
"It remembers," said Socrates.
"It forgives," Aristotle added with a grin.

They laughed together as the goat shook itself and
trotted toward the sound of its master's call.

The Return

The shepherd met them halfway down the path,
gratitude in his eyes.
"You caught her!" he exclaimed.

"Not caught," Socrates corrected gently. "We simply learned how to follow."

The man chuckled. "You talk like poets." He patted the goat's flank. "She's clever, this one—opens her own gate."
Aristotle's eyes lit up. "How?"
"With her horns," the man said proudly. "Hooks the latch and lifts. Took me days to figure out."

Plato laughed. "Then she's a philosopher too—seeking freedom."

The shepherd smiled. "If she is, may she learn wisdom before she learns to climb the roof again."

They all laughed, and the man led the goat back toward the village.

The Evening Walk

The three boys lingered by the stream as evening softened the hills.
The sky turned to gold, then rose, then violet. The smell of warm earth filled the air.

Plato skipped a stone across the water. "Do you think the goat knows what freedom is?"
Aristotle watched the ripples. "I think it feels something like it."

Socrates leaned back on his elbows. "Then perhaps feeling is the beginning of knowing."

Plato smiled. "Then maybe the world is full of thinkers who cannot speak."

"Or speakers who cannot think," said Aristotle, smirking.
Socrates laughed. "Then we must listen to both."

The night crickets began their slow, rhythmic song. A soft wind rustled the reeds.

Closing Reflection

Years later, the storyteller would tell of the day the boys chased a goat and found a question instead.
He would say that the creature, in its small rebellion, reminded them that life itself is wild thought—running, leaping, searching for an open gate.

And though the goat never spoke, its silence carried a lesson that words could not:
That the measure of understanding lies not in taming the world, but in meeting it without fear.

Chapter 5

The Secret Drawing

The Discovery

Morning light poured over the marble steps of the unfinished temple. Dust drifted in the sunbeams like tiny dancers, and the air smelled faintly of wet plaster and figs ripening in the nearby orchards.

Plato knelt in the courtyard with a stick, tracing shapes in the dust. His brow furrowed; each line curved and bent until it formed something between a circle and a cloud.

Aristotle leaned over his shoulder. "What is it supposed to be?"

Plato didn't look up. "Not supposed to be. It is."

"It looks like smoke."

"Maybe it is smoke."

Socrates, sitting a few steps above them, smiled. "Then perhaps beauty is what vanishes even as it's made."

Aristotle scoffed. "Beauty must be clear, not vague. A shape should stay still."

Plato looked at his drawing. "But clouds move, and they're still beautiful."

The Critique

Aristotle picked up another stick and began marking straight lines beside Plato's spirals. "See? Order. Proportion. That's what makes something right."

Socrates watched, amused. "You draw with rules; he draws with memory."

Aristotle frowned. "Rules keep things true."

"Then why," Socrates asked, "do they change when you grow older?"

The boy hesitated. "Because we see better."

Socrates nodded. "Then perhaps beauty grows with the eye that sees."

Plato glanced toward the sky. "Sometimes, I think beauty hides from the eyes that stare too hard."

The Secret

A breeze lifted the dust, smudging Plato's work. He pressed his palm over part of it, trying to protect the faint outline.

Aristotle tilted his head. "What's that you're hiding?"

"Nothing."

Socrates stood and walked down the steps. "Nothing is often something precious."

Plato hesitated, then brushed away part of the dust. Beneath the swirl was a small face—barely drawn, only eyes and a faint curve of a mouth.

Socrates crouched beside him. "Who is it?"

"My mother," Plato said softly. "She's been ill. I wanted to draw her as I remember, not as she looks now."

Aristotle's teasing stopped. "That's why you didn't want us to see."

Plato nodded. "It isn't perfect."

"Nothing living is," Socrates murmured. "Perfection is what life longs for, not what it is."

The Lesson in Form

The three sat quietly. The half-face in the dust seemed to breathe with the wind.

Socrates traced a circle around it. "The form protects the meaning," he said. "Just as the temple protects the prayer."

Aristotle studied the drawing. "So beauty isn't in how it looks, but in why it's made."

Plato smiled faintly. "Then maybe everything beautiful begins in a secret."

Socrates nodded. "A secret that wishes to be shared but fears to be misunderstood."

He looked at the temple walls rising behind them.

"Men will carve gods into these stones, thinking they capture the divine. Yet perhaps the divine is only the longing that makes them carve."

Aristotle considered this. "Then builders and artists are both seekers."

"And philosophers," said Socrates, "are the ones who ask what they seek."

The Experiment

Plato brushed a clear space on the ground. "Let's each draw something beautiful, and then we'll see what it means."

"Agreed," said Aristotle.

They began. Dust lifted and swirled as three different visions took shape.

Aristotle drew a perfect olive leaf, counting the veins and edges. "This is beauty because it's exact," he said proudly.

Plato drew a spiraling line that doubled back on itself, flowing like a gust of wind. "Mine moves. It's never finished."

Socrates stooped and drew a single circle, smooth and complete. "Mine contains both of yours. It is still, yet endless."

Aristotle laughed. "That's not fair—you drew the simplest thing!"

Socrates smiled. "Then why do men never tire of looking at it?"

Plato nodded thoughtfully. "Maybe beauty isn't what fills the space but what surrounds it."

The Argument of Light

A passing cloud dimmed the courtyard. The boys' drawings softened, losing shape.

"Now whose is most beautiful?" asked Socrates.

Aristotle squinted. "I can barely see mine."

"Mine's gone," said Plato. "It vanished."

Socrates traced the faint circle again with his toe. "And yet the idea of it remains. Beauty may fade from the dust, but not from the mind that saw it."

Plato's eyes brightened. "Then what we call beautiful is only the memory of perfection."

"Or the wish for it," said Socrates.

Aristotle looked puzzled. "But if beauty is only in the mind, then why do we build temples or paint or sing?"

"To remind the mind what it loves," Socrates answered.

The Moment of Understanding

From the temple came the sound of chisels. A sculptor was working inside, shaping a marble column.

They crept closer and peeked through the archway. The sculptor's hammer struck slowly, each tap releasing pale curls of stone. The column gleamed where sunlight touched it.

Plato whispered, "He's setting the spirit free."

Aristotle shook his head. "He's shaping it."

Socrates whispered back, "Perhaps both. The shaping is the freeing."

The man looked up, smiled at the boys, and said, "Stone remembers every hand that touches it."

When they returned to the courtyard, Plato looked at his faint drawing. "Then maybe dust remembers too."

"Then let it remember this day," said Socrates.

He smoothed his own circle until it disappeared. "Nothing truly beautiful is lost; it only changes form."

The Evening Sky

As dusk settled, the boys walked home through the olive groves. The sky glowed like burnished copper, and the air hummed with bees returning to their hives.

Aristotle carried a small branch of leaves. "I'll press these in my journal."

Plato smiled. "To keep beauty still?"

"To study it later."

Socrates looked toward the horizon. "Then study the silence too; it teaches as much as form."

They reached the hill overlooking the sea. The wind tugged at their hair, and the sun sank low, scattering light across the water like liquid glass.

Plato stopped walking. "Do you ever think light is what beauty looks like before it becomes anything else?"

Socrates nodded. "And darkness, perhaps, is what remains when beauty rests."

Aristotle laughed. "You both make my head spin."

"Then your thoughts are waking," said Socrates, smiling.

Closing Reflection

The storyteller, remembering the day, would say that Plato's first philosophy began not in a grand hall but in the dust of a courtyard. He would tell how a boy's hand, trembling with love and fear, drew the first imperfect line that reached toward the perfect.

He would say that in that secret drawing, hidden from the world, beauty found its first whisper of eternity—and that from such whispers, all the world's ideals are born.

Chapter 6

The Lost Coin

The Discovery

The morning sun spilled through the narrow streets of Athens, glinting off the bronze handles of shop doors and baskets filled with olives. The air smelled of bread, salt, and laughter.

Plato, Socrates, and Aristotle had agreed to help an old market vendor sweep the square after the morning rush. Stalls stood half-empty, the sound of brooms brushing stone echoing softly between them.

As Aristotle swept near the edge of a stall, something small flashed in the dust. He bent down and lifted a coin, its surface catching the light like a secret.

"Look!" he cried. "Fortune has smiled on me!"

Plato wiped his brow. "Maybe it smiled on someone else first."

Socrates raised an eyebrow. "And now, perhaps, it is testing you."

Aristotle laughed. "How can it be a test? It was just lying there!"

"Then so is truth," said Socrates gently, "but not all who find it know what to do with it."

The Dispute of Possession

They gathered around the coin. It was heavier than it looked, etched with the faint image of an owl—the mark of Athens itself.

"It's beautiful," said Plato. "But how do we know whose it was?"

Aristotle flipped it once in his hand. "It's mine now. The gods chose me to see it."

"Do the gods decide who sees," asked Socrates, "or who understands what he has seen?"

Aristotle frowned. "If you're saying it isn't mine, then whose is it?"

Plato thought for a moment. "Maybe it belongs to whoever misses it most."

"That's nonsense," Aristotle said. "Belonging is a matter of law."

"Then perhaps," Socrates replied, "the law of the heart is older than the law of the city."

Aristotle looked away. "You both make everything confusing."

"Only so we may see more clearly," Socrates said with a smile.

The Merchant's Story

As the boys continued sweeping, an old man stumbled into the square. His robe was dusty, and he peered at the ground as though searching for something fragile.

"Have you lost something, sir?" asked Plato.

The man sighed. "A small coin. Worth less than a loaf of bread, yet worth more than gold to me."

Aristotle's fingers tightened around the coin in his pocket. "Why is it worth so much?" he asked.

The man smiled faintly. "Because it was the last thing my wife gave me before she passed. She told me to keep it as a reminder that love, once given, never leaves us."

He looked toward the ground again. "I have searched since dawn, but perhaps the gods wished to keep it."

Socrates placed a hand on the man's shoulder. "Perhaps they wished to remind us that even the smallest loss can teach the greatest care."

The man nodded wearily and walked away, his sandals scraping against the stones.

The Quiet Conflict

The air felt different now—heavier. Aristotle stood apart, staring at the outline of his footprints.

Plato approached. "You're quiet."

"I was thinking," said Aristotle, "if I give it back, he'll think I stole it. But if I keep it, I'll know I did."

Socrates joined them. "Then the question is not what the man will think, but what you will remember."

Aristotle turned the coin in his palm. "What if goodness is only something people talk about, not something that really lives inside us?"

"Then you must prove it lives," said Socrates. "Not to me, not to the old man—to yourself."

Plato crouched beside them. "Maybe goodness is like a melody we once knew. We forget the notes until something makes us hum again."

Socrates smiled. "Then perhaps this coin is your song."

The Choice

The day wore on.

The market quieted, and the smell of honey cakes drifted from a nearby stall. The three boys sat beneath an awning, each lost in thought.

Aristotle held the coin tightly, feeling its cool weight. "I found it," he whispered.

"But it doesn't feel like mine anymore."

Socrates nodded. "Some things grow heavier the longer we carry them."

Plato leaned forward. "Then maybe letting go is the only way to keep them."

Aristotle stood suddenly. "I'm going to find the old man."

They followed as he walked through the winding streets, past pottery stands and spice shops. The sun had begun to lower, spilling gold over the rooftops.

When they reached the corner near the olive press, they saw the old man sitting alone, resting on a low wall.

Aristotle stepped closer. "Sir," he said quietly, "I think the gods wanted this to find its way back."

He held out the coin. The man looked at it, then at Aristotle's trembling hands.

"You found it?"

"Yes."

"And you return it freely?"

Aristotle nodded. "I think it belonged to more than you."

The man smiled, eyes glistening. "Then you have learned something rare. You have remembered."

He pressed the coin back into Aristotle's palm. "Keep it, boy. Let it remind you that goodness never truly leaves us—it only waits to be found again."

Aristotle froze. "But—"

The man rose and walked away before he could finish.

Socrates watched in silence. "It seems the gods have tested two hearts and found both worthy." As Socrates turned to look at the old man, a sudden breeze washed across his face.

The old man was gone.

The Evening Reflection

They walked home as the light faded. The coin gleamed faintly in Aristotle's hand, reflecting the last color of day.

Plato broke the silence. "Do you think he meant what he said? He spoke like a philosopher."

Socrates nodded. "He meant that goodness, once awakened, belongs to everyone."

Aristotle looked at the coin again. "I don't understand why it feels so different now."

"Because it has changed form," said Socrates. "It was once metal; now it is meaning."

Plato smiled. "Then goodness must be the soul remembering what it already knew."

Socrates nodded. "Exactly. Men call it virtue, but it is really memory."

Aristotle turned the coin over once more. "Then maybe every good thing we do is a piece of remembering."

"And every wrong thing," said Socrates, "is the forgetting."

The Lesson at Dusk

They stopped at the edge of the sea. Waves murmured against the rocks, soft as breath. The horizon burned orange, then violet.

Aristotle held the coin out toward the light. "It shines brighter now."

"Perhaps," said Plato, "because it has been seen by truth."

Socrates placed a hand on each of their shoulders. "The soul is not taught goodness; it recalls it. Every choice is a lesson in remembrance."

A gull cried overhead, swooping low and vanishing into the glow. The boys stood silent, watching until the light slipped away.

Closing Reflection

The storyteller would later say that the day of the lost coin was the day the boys learned what cannot be bought or sold. He would say that Aristotle, who once believed that value lay in the thing itself, began to glimpse the truth that value lives in the heart that knows its worth.

And he would tell his listeners that goodness is not a lesson given by others, but a whisper from within—a memory of light that even the dust of the world cannot cover.

Chapter 7

The Festival of Light

The Festival Begins

The first evening of midsummer filled Athens with song. The sea breeze carried the scent of roasted figs and sweet wine through the narrow streets.

Lamps were being hung from doorways and trees, and the whole city seemed to shimmer beneath their glow.

Socrates, Plato, and Aristotle helped the villagers hang garlands of olive leaves around the square. Each leaf caught a glimmer of light from the fires that danced along the hills.

Children laughed, dogs barked, and merchants called to one another across the music and clatter of cups.

Plato stopped to watch a line of torches being lit one by one. "It's like watching stars being born," he said softly.

"Or like the gods setting the world alight again," Aristotle replied, grinning.

Socrates smiled. "Then let us hope they do not forget to leave us a little darkness to rest in."

The Question of Joy

Later, when the torches burned low, the boys sat near the temple steps. The marble glowed orange from the firelight. Music drifted from the courtyard, a flute and drum keeping time with laughter.

Plato sighed. "Every festival feels like a dream. It shines so bright and then vanishes."

Aristotle looked at him. "That's because you think too much about the end. I'd rather enjoy the middle."

Socrates chuckled. "And I'd rather understand why joy visits us at all."

Plato tossed a fig into the air and caught it. "Maybe joy is just a trick of the gods—to keep us chasing it."

"Or," said Aristotle, "it comes from action. From doing something good."

Socrates leaned back against a column. "Then tell me, which lasts longer—the deed or the joy that follows?"

"The deed," said Aristotle quickly.

"Ah," Socrates smiled, "then joy must be the echo of virtue."

Plato nodded slowly. "An echo we spend our lives trying to hear again."

The Encounter

As the night deepened, the three wandered toward the harbor where lanterns floated above the water like captive moons. Near the steps of a small shrine, they heard the faint sound of a lyre.

A man sat there—old, blind, his eyes pale as marble. His fingers plucked the strings softly, weaving notes that seemed to hum within the soul rather than the ear.

The boys stood quietly, listening.

When the song ended, Aristotle stepped forward. "That was beautiful, sir. How do you play so well when you cannot see the strings?"

The man smiled. "Because I do not see the strings—I feel the song."

Plato asked, "Do you miss seeing the lights of the festival?"

The man shook his head. "I have never seen them. I was born in darkness."

Socrates lowered his voice. "And yet, you seem to know light better than most who live in it."

The man turned his face toward the sound of Socrates' voice. "The gods gave me ears to see what hearts cannot hide. I hear the light in laughter, the glow in silence, the fire in kindness. That is enough."

The Lesson of the Musician

They sat beside him as he tuned the lyre again. "Do you play every festival?" asked Plato.

"Every one," said the man. "My music helps others see what I cannot. In that way, I borrow their eyes."

Aristotle frowned thoughtfully. "Then perhaps beauty is not in seeing, but in sharing."

"Indeed," said the man. "Beauty is not in the thing itself, but in the harmony between giver and listener."

Socrates smiled. "Then the blind see through harmony, and the seeing are blind until they learn it."

The man nodded. "Light does not live in lamps, boys— it lives in what the light touches."

Plato whispered, "Then even the shadows serve it."

The old musician began another melody, slower, gentler, like water rippling around stones.

The notes rose and fell like a prayer. People nearby stopped to listen; even the sea seemed to quiet.

When the song ended, the man bowed his head. "Now go," he said softly. "The lanterns will soon rise, and the night will remember your faces."

The Lanterns Released

They joined the villagers at the shore. The tide shimmered with hundreds of small floating lamps, each resting on a leaf or bit of wood.

Children ran with laughter as their parents lit the wicks, whispering wishes to the sea. Plato, Aristotle, and Socrates stood side by side, each holding a lantern.

"What will you wish for?" asked Aristotle.

Plato smiled. "For truth—to see beyond what seems."

Socrates chuckled. "Ever the dreamer."

"And you?" asked Aristotle.

Socrates looked toward the horizon. "For peace—not the peace of silence, but the peace that follows understanding."

"And you, Aristotle?" asked Plato.

The youngest hesitated. "For knowledge, but not only to know, to use it well."

Socrates nodded approvingly. "Then our lanterns carry the same flame, though each burns for a different reason."

They set their lanterns gently onto the water. The waves caught them, carrying them slowly away until they joined the glowing trail of hundreds more drifting toward the open sea.

The Realization

The boys sat on the rocks watching their lanterns drift farther and farther, the wind rippling the reflections like liquid fire.

Aristotle broke the silence. "Do you think the gods see these lights?"

Socrates smiled. "If they do not, then perhaps they feel them."

Plato rested his chin on his knees. "It's strange—the lights look smaller as they float away, but somehow they seem greater too."

Socrates nodded. "So it is with goodness. When it leaves our hands, it grows beyond us."

Aristotle picked up a small stone and tossed it into the sea. "Then maybe life is like this water—each act sending ripples that touch others."

Plato turned toward him. "Then what makes a life worth living?"

Socrates leaned forward, watching the last of the lanterns fade toward the horizon. "Perhaps," he said quietly, "a life worth living is one that keeps the flame alive—even when the night returns."

They sat in silence for a long time, the wind cool on their faces, the sea breathing softly below.

The Journey Home

When the last fires dimmed, the boys began the walk back to the village. The streets were quiet now, scattered with petals and the faint scent of incense.

Aristotle looked up. "The stars look like lanterns too."

Plato nodded. "Maybe they are, the gods' own lights, drifting in the sky."

Socrates smiled. "Then we are all lanterns, carried by time, burning until the dawn."

They passed the old musician sitting again near the temple steps. He heard their footsteps and called out, "Did you send your lights to the sea?"

"We did," said Plato. "Each with a wish."

"Then the gods have seen you," said the man. "For every flame that leaves the shore lights another somewhere unseen."

They thanked him and continued walking. Socrates glanced back once, watching the man's fingers move across the lyre, though no sound followed—only the rhythm of memory.

Closing Reflection

Years later, the storyteller would wtite that the night of the Festival of Light was the night the three young philosophers learned what all men seek—not immortality, but illumination.

He would tell that the blind musician taught them that light is not what we see, but what we give. That truth, goodness, and beauty are but names for one flame, the flame of understanding that passes quietly from soul to soul.

And he would say that when the boys watched their lanterns drift into the dark, they did not know that one day their words, too, would become lanterns—floating through time, lighting the minds of generations yet unborn.

Chapter 8

The Empty Cup

The Potter's Shop

The air inside the potter's shop was warm and alive with motion. The wheel hummed like a low song as clay spun and rose beneath the craftsman's hands. Outside, the sun baked the streets of Athens, but here the air was cool and smelled of earth and smoke.

Socrates entered first, greeting the potter with a bow of the head. Plato and Aristotle followed, their sandals crunching over bits of dried clay scattered on the floor.

The potter's apprentice, a boy not much older than Aristotle, worked at the wheel with furrowed brow. He pressed his fingers too hard, and the clay collapsed in on itself.

"Again!" he muttered, slamming the lump back onto the wheel. "I'll never get it right."

The potter smiled patiently. "You will, when the clay stops fighting your hands."

The apprentice scowled. "It's the clay that doesn't listen."

Socrates folded his arms. "Ah, but perhaps it listens too well," he said.

The apprentice blinked. "How can clay listen?"

"When your hands are tense," said Socrates, "it becomes tense. When you rush, it hurries and falls."

The boy frowned and turned back to the wheel, muttering under his breath.

The Lesson in Patience

The philosopher watched quietly while the boys leaned closer to see.

The wheel turned again, faster this time. The clay began to rise, but then wobbled and collapsed once more. Water splashed across the table.

The apprentice groaned. "It keeps breaking!"

The potter sighed. "You push too much."

"I'm trying to make it perfect!"

Socrates stepped closer. "And in that trying, you forget to listen."

He turned to Plato and Aristotle. "Tell me, what do you see?"

Plato studied the misshapen lump. "It wasn't centered," he said. "It leaned as it turned."

Aristotle nodded. "And it was too thin at the base."

Socrates smiled. "Both true. Yet I see another flaw."

He looked at the boy's hands—stiff, impatient, trembling. "It lacked emptiness."

The apprentice frowned. "How can something lack emptiness?"

Socrates pointed toward the shelves lined with finished bowls, their curves smooth and shining in the light. "What makes those useful?"

"The shape," said the apprentice.

"The material," said Aristotle.

Socrates shook his head. "No. What makes them useful is the space inside. Without that emptiness, a cup is only a stone."

The apprentice looked uncertain. Plato tilted his head. "Then the nothing inside is what gives it purpose."

"Exactly," said Socrates. "And so it is with the mind."

The Demonstration

Socrates took one of the apprentice's cups from the table and filled it with water from a jug. He poured until the water spilled over, splashing onto the floor.

"See?" he said. "When a cup is full, nothing more can enter. The same is true of knowledge.

When one believes he already knows enough, wisdom has no room to dwell."

Aristotle smiled faintly. "So to learn, we must first be empty."

Plato added, "But emptiness feels like ignorance."

Socrates laughed softly. "Only to those who have not yet tasted learning. Ignorance is the refusal to see; emptiness is the readiness to receive."

The potter, listening from the back of the room, nodded in quiet agreement. "He speaks truth," he said. "A vessel cannot shape itself, and a proud student learns less than the clay."

The apprentice looked down at the wet floor. "Then how do I make myself empty?"

Socrates dipped his fingers into the spilled water and drew a small circle on the table.

"Begin by noticing what fills you—impatience, pride, fear. When you can name what clutters your mind, you can begin to clear it."

The boy stared at his ruined cup. "And if I fail again?"

Socrates smiled. "Then fail again, but this time, watch what your failure teaches."

The Riverbank

Later that afternoon, the boys left the village and walked toward the river. The air shimmered with heat. Cicadas droned in the trees, and the scent of wild thyme drifted through the air.

They sat beneath a fig tree near the water's edge, where the shade was cool. Plato skimmed a pebble across the surface; Aristotle dug a stick into the damp earth.

"I keep thinking about what he said," Plato began. "How can we empty the mind? Thoughts keep coming even when we don't want them."

Socrates smiled. "The river never stops flowing either, yet it remains clear because it does not try to hold what passes."

Aristotle frowned. "But how can we learn if we forget what we think?"

Socrates plucked a reed from the bank and held it up.

"Does this reed remember the water that once passed through it?"

"No," said Aristotle.

"Yet it sings because of it," Socrates said, blowing gently across the hollow stem. A soft tone sounded in the air. "It does not cling to the breath; it gives it voice."

Plato leaned forward. "Then the mind must be like that reed—open, letting thoughts move through instead of keeping them."

"Precisely," said Socrates. "To know is not to collect but to connect—to see how every idea breathes into another."

Aristotle smiled. "That means we should think less of what we hold and more of what we let go."

Socrates nodded. "True wisdom often begins with surrender."

The Broken Cup

When the sun began to sink, the apprentice from the potter's shop appeared on the path, carrying a small clay cup. He saw the three figures by the river and hurried to them.

"Socrates!" he called. "I brought this to show you."

He held up the cup. Its surface was uneven, and a crack ran along one side.

"I tried again," the boy said. "It's still not perfect."

Socrates took the cup and turned it gently in his hands. The clay was rough, but the shape held firm. He smiled. "Tell me what you learned."

The boy hesitated. "That the clay doesn't hurry for me."

"And what else?"

"That if I keep my hands light, it listens better."

Socrates nodded. "Then the cup has already served its purpose."

"But it's cracked," the boy said.

Socrates dipped the cup into the river and lifted it, water streaming through the fracture in narrow silver threads. "Yet see—though it cannot hold everything, it still carries something.

Even a broken vessel can serve truth if it remains humble."

Plato watched the water dripping from the cup. "Then perhaps the cracks are what make us need one another."

Socrates smiled. "Indeed. Perfection isolates; imperfection binds."

Aristotle gazed at the river. "So being empty doesn't mean being nothing—it means being ready."

Socrates nodded. "And readiness is the beginning of wisdom."

The apprentice bowed his head. "Then I will keep this one as it is—to remind me."

The Evening Return

They walked back toward the village together. The air cooled, and the smell of wood smoke rose from the houses. The sky deepened into violet.

Socrates carried the cracked cup in his hands, as if it were something sacred. "Remember," he said, "emptiness is not a flaw to fix, but a door to keep open."

Plato looked thoughtful. "Then every question we ask is another doorway."

"And every answer," added Aristotle, "a key that opens it."

Socrates smiled. "Yes—but the wise remember to keep walking after the door opens."

As they reached the edge of the market square, they passed the potter's shop. The old craftsman stood in the doorway, wiping his hands. Seeing them, he lifted a finished cup into the fading light. Its surface gleamed, the inside shadowed and deep.

"Empty, yet complete," he said.

Socrates bowed. "As all wisdom should be."

Closing Reflection

The storyteller would later say that on that day, the young philosophers learned that wisdom begins not with knowing, but with the courage to unlearn.

He would say that the cracked cup still rests somewhere in Athens, its hollow heart filled only with the silence that listens—and that from such silence, all true understanding is born.

Chapter 9

The Thread and the Loom

The Weaver's Courtyard

The day began with the smell of wet wool and crushed lavender. In a narrow courtyard behind the market, skeins of dyed yarn hung from a rope like small sunsets—crimson, saffron, indigo—dripping quietly into clay bowls.

A wooden loom stood near the shade of a fig tree, its frame worn smooth by years of patient hands.

Socrates led the way in, with Plato beside him and Aristotle trailing a few paces behind, distracted by a fat bee bumping its head against the fig leaves.

The weaver, a silver-haired woman with eyes the color of the Aegean, glanced up and smiled without stopping her work.

"You've come to watch?" she asked, passing a shuttle through the warp with a gentle flick.

The loom answered with a soft wooden thrum—thread, wood, breath, and time keeping an old rhythm together.

"To learn," Socrates replied. "If you are willing."

"The loom is a willing teacher," she said. "It never lies. Sit, and listen to it."

The First Pattern

They settled on low stools. The courtyard hummed with cicadas; somewhere beyond the wall a goat bleated, as if offering commentary. Plato watched the shuttle travel back and forth, the pattern slowly appearing like a secret rising to the surface.

"It looks like a river," Plato said softly. "But the river is made of lines."

Aristotle leaned toward the loom. "What makes the lines hold?"

"The warp," the weaver said, tapping the taut vertical threads. "They are fixed. The weft travels across them, over and under, carrying color. Without the warp, the cloth has no spine.

Socrates folded his hands. "And without the hands?"

"Then all the threads would remain only threads," she answered, eyes twinkling. "A world of maybe, never becoming."

The Quarrel of Choice

Aristotle frowned. "If the warp is fixed, does that mean the pattern is decided before you begin?"

"Some is decided," she said. "The width, the strength, the borders. But the path of color is mine to guide." She held up the shuttle. "And sometimes the thread surprises even me."

Plato smiled. "Then fate is the frame, and freedom is the thread."

"Or fate is the thread," Aristotle countered, "and freedom is the hand."

Socrates asked, "Which of you will be angrier if the cloth turns out different than you expected?"

They laughed. The weaver's shuttle slid again, whispering across the warp like a small boat crossing a calm bay.

The Knot

As the pattern grew, a thin knot appeared in the indigo strand. The weaver paused. "There," she murmured. "A stubborn place."

Aristotle leaned closer. "Will it ruin the cloth?"

"Only if I pretend it isn't there," she said.

With a pin, she gentled the knot into the shelter of a crossing thread. The warp accepted it, the pattern swallowed it, and the cloth continued.

Plato watched, thoughtful. "So even flaws can be woven into meaning."

"More than that," said the weaver. "Some patterns are too smooth to be believed. A small roughness tells the hand it is touching something real."

The Boy with the Red Cord

A shadow crossed the gate. A boy not much older than Aristotle stood there, clutching a coil of bright red cord. His hair was wind-tossed, his sandals dusty.

"Mistress," he said awkwardly, "my mother sent me to ask—can you add this to my father's cloak? He returns from the road tonight. She wants the hem mended with our family color."

The weaver took the cord and weighed it in her palm. "It will stand out," she said. "Red speaks loudly."

The boy flushed. "He is a loud man. But kind."

Socrates glanced at Plato and Aristotle, then back to the boy. "What is your father called?"

"People call him 'Bull'," the boy said, with equal parts pride and embarrassment. "But his given name is Nikias."

Plato grinned. "Then he has two names—a name for the world and a name for home."

Socrates nodded. "And which one is truer?"

The boy hesitated. "When he is angry, he is Bull. When he laughs, he is Nikias."

"Then perhaps a man is a pattern of both," Socrates said gently. "Loudness and kindness woven together."

The weaver threaded the red through the shuttle. "Sit," she told the boy. "If this cord belongs in your father's cloak, let it be placed by his son's watching."

The Test of the Warp

Aristotle could not help himself. "How strong is the warp?" he asked. "Can it be measured?"

"By strain and time," the weaver said. "Pull too tight, and the threads break; leave them slack, and the pattern sags."

Socrates raised an eyebrow. "And in men?"

"The same," she replied. "A life pulled too tight breaks; too slack, and nothing holds.

Good hands know the difference."

Plato traced a finger just above the cloth, not touching. "The spaces between the threads—do they matter?"

"They give breath," the weaver said. "Cloth without air suffocates its wearer."

Socrates smiled. "So even absence has work to do."

The Walk to the Dye Vats

When the sun climbed to its hottest, the weaver set the shuttle aside. "Come," she said. "If you are to understand, you must see color being made."

She led them along a narrow path to a shed where two dye vats steamed faintly—one a dark vat that smelled of vinegar and smoke, the other sweet with crushed leaves.

Plato wrinkled his nose. "Beauty begins in strange places."

"Often," the weaver agreed. "We dip what is pale into what looks like soot, and it rises colored like evening."

Aristotle peered over the lip of the indigo vat. "Why does it change color in the air?"

"Because the air finishes what the water begins," she said. "What is hidden becomes visible when it meets the world."

Socrates looked at the boys. "Remember that."

She lowered a skein into the vat. For a moment it looked bruised and dull.

Then, as it lifted and caught the light, blue bloomed along its length like dawn rushing up a hillside.

Plato's eyes widened. "It is as if the thread remembers the sky."

"Or as if the sky recognizes the thread," Socrates said.

A Question of Names

Back in the courtyard, the red cord lay coiled like a small flame. The boy watched the loom with solemn devotion.

"What is your name?" Plato asked him.

"Damon," he said. "But some call me 'Little Bull'."

Aristotle grinned. "Do you like that?"

Damon kicked at a pebble. "I think I must earn it. But I do not wish to be angry to do so."

Socrates leaned forward. "Then perhaps earn the other part—the kindness."

Damon looked relieved, as if someone had lifted a stone from his chest. "How do I do that?"

"Begin where you are," Socrates said. "Your mother sent you with a task. Complete it with care. The name will follow the deed."

The weaver nodded. "Names are threads. If we tug them too hard, they tangle. If we ignore them, they fray. Work them into the pattern by the life you live."

The Choice of the Border

The weaver paused after several passes of red. "The hem needs a border," she said. "A narrow band to keep the edge from unraveling."

"Can a border be beautiful?" Plato asked. "Or is it only a fence?"

"Both," she said. "A good border holds the world together without choking it."

Socrates turned to Aristotle. "In argument, what serves as a border?"

Aristotle thought. "Definitions," he said at last. "If we do not say what we mean, our words fall apart."

"And in friendship?" Socrates asked Damon.

The boy's brow furrowed. "Promises," he said slowly. "When we do what we said we would."

Socrates smiled. "Then truth is a border that keeps love from unraveling." Plato nodded, storing the sentence like a pebble with an unusual shine.

The Tear

A sudden rip sounded—soft, but sharp enough to draw breath from every mouth.

The warp had snapped along the edge where the red band began. The weaver's hands were already upon it, stilling the threads.

"I did this," Damon whispered, stricken. "I asked for red."

"No," the weaver said calmly. "Threads break. That is their nature. Watch."

With a bone needle she gathered the loose ends, eased them into a small, deliberate knot, and worked the knot into the border itself. "If the break is near the edge," she said, "we do not hide it in the middle. We strengthen the edge with it."

Aristotle exhaled. "So a fault becomes a brace."

"Exactly." She smoothed the cloth, then resumed the patient rhythm of weaving. The loom answered with its quiet thrum, as if nothing had happened.

Socrates looked at the boys. "Let that be a lesson you do not forget."

The Noon Bread

They ate flatbread with olives while the loom murmured on. Damon told small stories about his father—how he sang loudly in the mornings and fell asleep in the doorway after long trips, shoes still dusty.

"He sounds like a festival," Plato said, smiling.

"Sometimes too loud," Damon admitted. "But when he carries me on his shoulders, the city looks like a map."

Aristotle wiped his hands. "Maps are only lines until someone walks them."

Socrates nodded. "And names are only sounds until someone lives them." Damon sat straighter at that, like a sparrow finding its balance on a fence.

The Gift

When the hem was finished, the weaver trimmed the ends and smoothed the cloth with her palm. She held the cloak up; the red border caught the light, bright as pomegranate seeds.

"Take this home," she told Damon, laying the cloak across his arms. "Tell your mother the border is strong."

The boy looked torn between gratitude and worry. "What do I pay you?"

"Bring me a story the next time you come," she said. "Two, if they are short."

Damon laughed, relief bright in his eyes. "I can do that."

He bowed to the weaver, then to the three friends, and hurried away—red flashing against white as he turned the corner toward home.

The Question the Loom Asked

The afternoon leaned toward gold. Shadows of fig leaves dappled the courtyard floor. The loom kept time.

Socrates rose. "You have been generous," he told the weaver. "You have taught us more than threads."

"Threads are only lines wanting meaning," she said. "Men give them that."

Plato hesitated. "May we ask one last thing?"

The weaver nodded.

"If a pattern begins one way," Plato said, "can it be changed?"

She rested a hand on the warp. "Not without cost. You must unweave what has been done. It takes patience, and in the end the cloth may be thinner for it."

Aristotle considered this. "But it can be done."

"It can," she said. "Better to see the pattern early, and choose well at the start."

Socrates' gaze softened. "And if a man has begun badly?"

The weaver looked at him—long enough that even the cicadas seemed to pause.

"Then let him begin again," she said, "and treat the new border as sacred."

Socrates bowed his head, as if receiving a private blessing.

The Road Home

They walked back through the thinning heat, past the dye shed and the goat whose bell now sounded like a memory.

Plato carried a thin strand of indigo the weaver had given him; Aristotle tucked a broken piece of shuttle into his belt like a treasure of wood.

"I think I understand," Aristotle said suddenly. "Causes are like warp and weft. Some causes are fixed—like the frame of the loom. Others move—like the shuttle's path."

Plato swung the indigo thread between finger and thumb so it flashed in the sun. "And ideas are like patterns that keep returning, no matter how the colors change."

Socrates smiled. "Then what are we?"

"Hands," Plato said.

"Eyes," said Aristotle.

"Breath," Socrates murmured. "Hands, eyes, and breath—the making of a life."

They stopped at the shade of an olive tree above the road. A breeze lifted the leaves; silver flashed like small fish in a green sea.

Plato tied the indigo to a twig. "A reminder," he said. "That choice must meet what is given."

Aristotle rubbed the shuttle-chip smooth with his thumb. "And that strength needs shape."

Socrates looked toward the city—white walls, red roofs, blue sea—and his face, for a heartbeat, held a distance the boys did not notice.

Closing Reflection

Years later, the storyteller would say that on the day of the loom the boys first felt the weight and mercy of design. He would say that they learned to honor borders not as prisons but as promises; to welcome flaws not as shame but as warning; to choose colors with care and to love the cloth that became of their days.

He would tell his listeners that fate is not a chain but a frame, and that freedom is not a shout but a steady hand—passing the shuttle back and forth until a pattern appears that even time will recognize.

Chapter 10

The Garden of Questions
The Hidden Gate

The road led them beyond the marketplace, past the olive presses and the clay kilns where red dust rose like memory.

At the edge of the city, half hidden behind a low stone wall, an archway of vine and ivy framed a narrow path. Socrates stopped, sensing quiet beyond the leaves.

"Here," he said, and brushed aside a trailing branch. The scent of rosemary and tilled earth drifted toward them. Within lay a small garden—a patchwork of green and brown, soft with sunlight and the faint murmur of bees.

An old man was bent over a row of lettuce, turning soil with a wooden spade. His beard was white, and his tunic stained with the honest marks of work. When he saw them, he leaned on the spade and smiled.

"Visitors? Few come this far unless they're lost or curious."

"We are both," Socrates replied.

The old man chuckled. "Then you'll fit right in. Here, we grow both kinds."

The Gardener's Wisdom

They followed him through narrow rows where mint brushed against their knees. Water glimmered in a small channel, carrying the reflection of the sky. Plato crouched beside it, dipping his fingers into the cool stream.

"It feels alive," he said.

"It is," the gardener replied. "The water listens to gravity and obeys, yet it nourishes freely.

Tell me—does that make it servant or master?"

Aristotle frowned, considering. "Neither. It is part of something larger. Its purpose is shared."

The gardener's eyes lit with approval. "A fine answer. The roots would agree."

Socrates smiled faintly. "You speak as though the soil has a soul."

"Perhaps it does," said the man. "Perhaps it only lends part of ours back to us when we walk upon it."

Seeds and Thought

The gardener motioned to a shaded bench beneath a fig tree. Beside it stood a wooden box filled with small clay bowls. Within each bowl lay seeds—some round, some flat, some speckled with color.

"Choose one," he said.

Plato picked a smooth, ivory seed. Aristotle chose a small brown one shaped like a tear. Socrates held a seed so tiny it nearly vanished in his palm.

"Each will grow into what it was meant to be," the gardener said. "But tell me—what do you think you hold?"

"A beginning," said Plato.

"A possibility," said Aristotle.

Socrates turned the seed in his fingers. "A question," he said. "One that only time can answer."

The gardener's smile deepened. "Then plant them, and may your answers have patience."

They pressed their seeds into the warm earth. The soil accepted them without complaint, the way wisdom accepts silence before speech.

The Circle of Growth

Later, they walked the length of the garden. Rows of young plants reached for the sun; vines trailed from trellises like careful handwriting. The gardener paused beside a patch of beans where wooden stakes rose in tidy lines.

"Do you see these stakes?" he asked. "They do not bear fruit, yet without them the vines would crawl and rot. Even what does not grow must guide what does."

Aristotle bent to touch the soil around one stake. "So structure gives shape to freedom."

"Exactly," said the gardener. "The world is full of such partnerships—roots and rain, shade and bloom, thought and deed."

Plato looked up at the tall fig tree nearby. "And man and the gods?"

The old man's eyes followed his gaze. "Ah. That depends who is holding the stake."

Socrates smiled at that, his eyes glimmering with amusement. "And sometimes, who is being held by it."

The Lesson of Waiting

They sat in silence for a while, the hum of bees filling the pause between thoughts. Then the gardener spoke again.

"You planted your seeds. What do you expect to see tomorrow?"

Plato answered first. "A sprout, perhaps."

Aristotle shook his head. "The soil needs time."

"And you?" the gardener asked Socrates.

Socrates folded his hands. "Expectation is the shadow of desire. I prefer surprise."

The gardener laughed softly. "A philosopher's patience. Still, even the patient man must water." He handed them a small jug. "Understanding is no different—it grows by care, not by staring."

Plato poured carefully, watching the water darken the soil. "So we must feed our thoughts as we feed these seeds."

"And guard them," added Aristotle. "Weeds are ideas that grow too fast."

Socrates looked up at the sky. "Then let us learn to recognize which thoughts belong."

Roots and Shadows

By midday the sun lay heavy across the garden. The gardener led them to a shaded arbor where a vine curled upward around a weathered column. At its base, roots wound deep into the soil.

"Look closely," he said. "The vine rises because it clings. It does not resist the column—it uses it."

Plato touched the bark like stem. "So strength can borrow from stillness."

"And stillness," said Aristotle, "can lend purpose to motion."

Socrates leaned against the column. "So a man rises not by refusing help, but by joining with what steadies him."

The gardener nodded. "Pride digs shallow roots. Gratitude reaches deep."

The Argument of the Ants

At their feet, a line of ants carried crumbs across a cracked stone path. Plato knelt, watching them disappear beneath a leaf.

"They work as though they share one mind," he said.

"Do they?" Aristotle asked. "Or is it only that they share one purpose?"

"Perhaps both," said Socrates. "Purpose gives form to mind."

The gardener listened, amused. "So, young philosophers, tell me—who leads them?"

They watched in silence. There was no leader, no signal, only movement—an unspoken order shaped by need.

"Then perhaps wisdom," Socrates said, "is knowing when not to lead."

"Or when to listen," replied Plato.

Aristotle brushed the dirt from his hands. "And when to carry the smallest piece."

The gardener smiled. "You've learned more from ants than most men do from books."

The Seedling's Lesson

They returned to where they had planted their seeds. Nothing had changed, and yet everything had. The soil looked richer where it had been watered. Plato crouched beside his patch, fingers sifting through the loose earth.

"It feels different," he said. "As though something beneath is awake."

"That is because it is," the gardener said. "Growth begins unseen. The roots work in darkness long before the leaf greets the light."

"So thought begins before words," murmured Socrates.

"Yes," the gardener said. "And the wisest speech remembers its roots."

Aristotle looked thoughtful. "If roots grow downward and leaves upward, then knowledge must have direction."

"It has purpose," the gardener said. "But not all direction is progress. A tree may grow tall and still be hollow."

"Then what makes growth good?" Plato asked.

"That which bears fruit for others," the gardener replied simply. "Selfish growth chokes the garden."

They sat quietly, letting the truth of it settle like dust after wind.

Evening Reflections

The day waned. The garden glowed gold beneath the sinking sun. The gardener offered them bread and figs, and they ate while cicadas began their slow song.

"You three remind me of seasons," he said. "Socrates, you are autumn—ripe with reflection. Plato, you are spring—bursting with new shapes of thought. Aristotle, you are summer—orderly and full of reason."

"And winter?" Socrates asked.

The gardener smiled. "Winter is the silence that waits for your return."

They bowed in gratitude. Plato looked reluctant to leave, his eyes wandering back to the patch of soil where his seed slept.

"You will not see it tomorrow," the gardener said. "But it will remember your hands."

"Do seeds remember?" Aristotle asked.

"Everything that seeks light remembers," the gardener said. "Even men."

The Road at Dusk

They left as the horizon dimmed into violet. The road wound between olive groves, their leaves whispering secrets in the breeze. The air smelled of dust and rosemary.

"What do you think he meant," Plato asked, "by the silence that waits for our return?"

"That thought never ends," Socrates said. "Only pauses, like a breath."

"Or like winter," Aristotle added. "A stillness that prepares for spring."

They walked without speaking for a while, listening to their footsteps mingle with the hum of crickets.

"The seed was small," Plato said softly. "Yet it holds a forest."

"Then guard your forest well," Socrates answered.

They passed beneath an arch of flowering laurel. Behind them, the last light of the day rested upon the garden wall like a promise.

Ahead, the road stretched open toward the unseen. And somewhere in the soft dark earth, three seeds dreamed of the sun.

Closing Reflection

Years later, the storyteller would say that wisdom often begins in gardens, not libraries. He would say that thought must be planted before it can bloom, and that silence is the rain from which understanding grows.

He would tell his listeners that the measure of growth is not height, but nourishment—that one should live as trees do, offering shade to those who follow. And when his story ended, he would smile and add that even the smallest seed contains an echo of eternity.

Chapter 11

The Philosopher's Promise

The Morning After

The morning after the Festival of Light was quieter than any dawn the boys could remember.

The air smelled faintly of smoke and sea salt. Tiny blackened shells of lanterns floated on the water like memories refusing to sink.

Socrates sat by the shore, his sandals resting in the damp sand. The waves rolled in and out, whispering secrets in a language older than thought.

Plato and Aristotle approached slowly, still half-dreaming from the night before.

"The lights are gone," said Aristotle.

Socrates smiled. "No, only changed. Fire does not vanish—it travels."

Plato followed his gaze. "Where does it travel to?"

"To wherever it is needed most," said Socrates. "Even to minds not yet born."

The Discussion of Endings

They sat together, watching the sunrise break through a thin veil of mist. The golden light spread across the sea like spilled honey.

Plato spoke first. "Socrates, how do we know when a lesson is finished?"

Socrates took a small pebble and tossed it into the water. Ripples spread outward, fading but never truly ending. "When it begins again in another."

Aristotle frowned. "Then no lesson ever ends."

Socrates nodded. "Not if it was worth learning."

Plato thought for a long moment. "And what if no one listens?"

"Then wisdom waits," said Socrates. "Truth does not depend on voices—it depends on time."

A gull flew overhead, calling out against the wind. Aristotle looked after it. "Do you think knowledge can outlive the body?"

Socrates' eyes brightened. "Knowledge is like the sea—it borrows shape from every shore, but it belongs to none. What we leave behind are waves, not footprints."

The Departure

They returned to the village, where a few merchants were already opening their stalls. The air carried the soft creak of wooden doors, the rattle of carts, the hum of a waking world.

Socrates stopped near the edge of the market square. "My time with you here grows short," he said. "Another city waits, and with it, new questions."

Plato's heart sank. "You're leaving?"

"For a little while." Socrates smiled faintly. "Wisdom does not sit still, and neither should we."

Aristotle kicked at the dust. "Will you come back?"

"Perhaps not to this place," said Socrates, "but in thought, always."

He reached into his robe and drew out three small objects—a smooth pebble, a slender reed, and a tiny feather. He handed the pebble to Aristotle. "For endurance—wisdom must stand firm."

He gave the reed to Plato. "For thought—wisdom must bend without breaking."

Finally, he held up the feather. "And for myself, a reminder that freedom is the lightest thing we carry."

The boys stood in silence, holding their gifts as though they were treasures.

The Last Walk

They followed him to the olive grove just beyond the hill. Dew glistened on the leaves like glass. The air was heavy with the scent of earth and sea, the same air that had carried their laughter and arguments through so many days.

Socrates stopped beside an old tree whose roots had broken through the ground like the veins of time itself.

"Every question you have asked," he said, "has been a branch from this same root. You may wander, but you will always return to the tree."

Plato traced the bark with his fingers. "Will we ever understand everything?"

Socrates smiled. "If understanding were complete, there would be no reason to think, and thought itself would die. The gods gave us wonder so that we might never grow tired of seeking."

Aristotle looked toward the path leading down the hill. "And what of those who forget to seek?"

Socrates picked up a fallen olive leaf and held it to the light. "Then the world waits for new seekers to remind them. That is how wisdom survives."

The Promise

The wind shifted, carrying the sound of distant bells from the harbor. Socrates looked out over the fields, his robe fluttering softly in the breeze.

"You will go farther than I," he said. "Your questions will grow beyond mine. But wherever wisdom leads you, remember this: walk humbly, and speak gently.

For truth bends like light; it does not end—it continues."

Plato looked at him with quiet awe. "How will we know if we have stayed on the right path?"

Socrates placed a hand on each of their shoulders. "When your words lift others rather than silence them. When you find joy not in being right, but in seeking what is right. When your thoughts make the world kinder, not smaller."

Aristotle nodded, clutching the pebble. "Then perhaps one day, others will walk beside us as we walk beside you."

Socrates' eyes shone. "That is the way of it. The torch passes, and with it, the warmth of every hand that carried it."

The Farewell

They walked back toward the village in silence. The sun had climbed higher, gilding the white walls and terracotta roofs with light. At the gate where the road curved away, Socrates turned and looked at them one last time.

"Do not mourn parting," he said. "It is the proof that you have loved what was worth keeping."

He began down the dusty road, his figure growing smaller against the brightness.

The breeze carried the faint echo of his voice: "Remember—seek truth, but never forget to live."

The boys stood for a long while, neither speaking. Then Plato whispered, "He walks toward another question."

Aristotle smiled sadly. "And we remain with his answers."

They turned back toward the olive grove, the morning light warming their faces.

The Reflection

That evening, as the first stars appeared, the boys sat beneath the same tree. The sea shimmered faintly in the distance.

Plato held the reed to his lips, listening to the soft whisper it made when the wind passed through it. "It sounds like him," he said.

Aristotle turned the pebble over in his hand. "He said it would endure. Maybe so will we."

They looked up as the stars brightened, countless lanterns hung by unseen hands.

Plato spoke quietly. "Perhaps the gods keep their own festival each night, to remind us that light never ends."

Aristotle nodded. "Then maybe wisdom is their fire, and we are its sparks."

Closing Reflection

The storyteller concludes that wisdom is a torch passed from hand to hand, but a flame that leaps of its own will from heart to heart and from age to age. It is a reflection the storyteller will hold for eternity.

Final Chapter

The Philosopher's Chamber

The Chamber Beyond Time

There exists a place where time has no measure, where neither the sun nor the stars mark its passing. It is the Philosopher's observatory—an eternal chamber of silence. A vast stone table stands at its center, carved from the same essence as thought itself.

Upon it rests a great open book, its pages shimmering faintly as though written in light. A single quill lies poised between the Philosopher's fingers, moving with patient grace.

Around him, shadows stretch infinitely, yet there is no darkness—only the dim, even glow of knowing. The air hums with the faint resonance of every question ever spoken, as if thought itself breathes here.

The Philosopher writes.

His hand moves slowly across the page, inscribing words that appear like ripples upon water. Each sentence glows briefly before fading into the parchment, becoming one with all that has been and all that will be. In this chamber, every thought that has ever been born finds its echo, and every echo finds its rest.

But tonight, the Philosopher pauses. His quill stills. The faint sound of his breath seems to fill the boundless hall. He looks up. Before him, standing half in shadow and half in light, are three figures—silent, watchful, patient.

They have been there all along.

Socrates. Plato. Aristotle.

The Philosopher's gaze softens. He closes the book with a gentle sound that seems to reverberate through eternity.

"You three old friends," he says quietly, "have waited long and patiently. Tell me, what have you learned?"

Socrates Speaks

The eldest steps forward, the light tracing the silver of his hair. His eyes carry the calm of one who has walked far within his own thoughts.

"As a child," he begins, "I was filled with questions— countless questions. Yet always there was a voice, faint but steady, that guided me toward reason. I could never see the one who spoke, but I felt him near, as though thought itself wished to teach me."

The Philosopher nods, saying nothing.

Plato Speaks

The second man steps forward. His face is neither old nor young, his eyes deep as the still sea.

"I, too, remember," he says. "As a boy, I questioned all things—truth, beauty, justice—and I feared that the world might offer no answers. Yet there was always another question waiting for me, as if the heavens themselves wished me to look deeper. I did not know from where it came, but it pulled me toward harmony, toward the unseen pattern of all things."

He lowers his head slightly, his tone softening. "It was through that quiet voice that I began to dream of worlds beyond this one."

Aristotle Speaks

The youngest steps from the shadow. His eyes are bright with thought, his face lit by an energy the others have tempered only with time.

"Then we are brothers of the same wonder," he says. "I, too, questioned everything and even doubted my own reason. But there was always a voice—not to answer, but to ask again—sharper, wiser, urging me to understand. Perhaps that voice was not outside me, but within all of us. A spark passed from mind to mind."

The Philosopher smiles faintly, as if the words confirm what he has always known.

The Philosopher's Reply

He rests his hand upon the great book.

"In this book," he says, "are all questions that have ever been asked—and those that shall be. The questions of your youth were written here long before your first breath.

The doubts you carried, the insights you shared—they were already part of this record. You were never alone in your wondering."

He looks toward them with quiet affection.

"Those children whom you have seen—they came here because of the questions they dared to ask. And now, those same three stand before me. You have walked through the pages of your own becoming."

The Philosopher's eyes gleam faintly in the still light. "You three, as children, had never met in the physical sense," he continues, "yet through thought—through the desire for questions and the longing for understanding—you found resonance in one another.

What binds you is not place, nor time, but the frequency of seeking itself. Each of your minds became an echo within the others, and in that harmony, wisdom was born."

The three philosophers bow their heads in quiet recognition. The silence that follows is not absence, but fullness.

The Book of Questions

The Philosopher turns the heavy cover once more, and the pages open by themselves.

Across them shimmer faint scenes—the well, the grove, the river, the village—the lives of children forever caught in inquiry. Their laughter, their doubts, their innocence flow together like light through crystal.

"These," he says, "were your beginnings.

Every question asked in purity is eternal. It returns again and again in new voices, in new minds, in every age that dares to seek."

He runs his hand gently along the open page. "In each generation, a child asks the same question as the first philosopher. And so, wisdom does not age; it only changes its language."

Socrates steps nearer to the book. "Then what becomes of our words?"

"They join the chorus," says the Philosopher. "Every truth spoken adds to the song of understanding. Every doubt adds harmony. And when a question is asked with honesty, the universe listens."

The Weight of Continuity

The Philosopher turns his gaze to them once more. "You have each shaped the world in your way. Yet what endures is not your names, but the spirit that moves through you—the spirit that questions without fear."

He closes the book softly, and the air seems to tremble. "The time will come when your words fade into dust, your scrolls crumble, and even your temples fall. But the resonance of your thought will continue—echoing in minds yet unborn.

The child who dares to ask 'Why?' will be your truest heir."

A gentle smile touches his lips. "For every question reborn keeps the world alive."

The Eternal Table

The Philosopher rises slowly from his seat. The great stone table glows faintly beneath his touch, its surface engraved with symbols that seem to shift and breathe. The book lies closed at its center, but the light within it does not dim. Around them, the chamber deepens into stillness.

"Remember this," he says. "Wisdom is not a possession to keep, but a flame that leaps of its own will—from heart to heart, from age to age. It does not belong to any man, yet it passes through all who listen."

The three men stand in silence, their faces illuminated by the glow of the table. They understand that this place is not merely a hall of thought—it is the inner chamber of every mind that dares to wonder.

The Departure

Socrates steps forward. "Then our purpose is not to hold wisdom, but to awaken it."

"Indeed," the Philosopher replies. "To awaken it, and to honor it. For the truest philosopher does not seek to be right—only to be open."

Plato speaks next. "And when we are gone?"

The Philosopher gestures to the book. "Then others will write. The flame will move, unseen but unbroken."

Aristotle's gaze lingers on the quill. "And you, Master—will you remain here forever?"

The Philosopher's eyes lift to the unseen stars above. "As long as there are questions, I shall remain. When the last question is silenced, creation itself will fall still."

He places the quill upon the table and rests both hands atop the book. "But that day will never come—for curiosity is infinite."

The Circle Complete

The chamber begins to brighten, the walls dissolving into light. The three philosophers seem less like men and more like reflections—thoughts taking form before fading back into the source. The Philosopher watches them go, his expression calm, his purpose complete.

He whispers, "All thought returns to its beginning."

And with that, the chamber falls silent again. Only the faint sound of a quill can be heard—somewhere, on another page, beginning to write anew.

Closing Reflection

The storyteller concludes that wisdom is not a light to be kept, but a flame that leaps of its own will—from heart to heart, and from age to age. It is a reflection the storyteller will hold for eternity.

www.ingramcontent.com/pod-product-compliance
Lightning Source LLC
Chambersburg PA
CBHW071233170626
46809CB00008BA/3033